PowerKids Readers:

The Bilingual Library of the United States of America™

Bilingual Edition
English/Spanish
Edición bilingüe

SOUTH CAROLINA
CAROLINA DEL SUR

JENNIFER WAY

TRADUCCIÓN AL ESPAÑOL: MARÍA CRISTINA BRUSCA

The Rosen Publishing Group's
PowerKids Press™ & **Editorial Buenas Letras**™
New York

Published in 2006 by The Rosen Publishing Group, Inc.
29 East 21st Street, New York, NY 10010

First Edition

Photo Credits: Cover © Tony Roberts/Corbis; p.p. 5, 25, 26, 30 (Capital) © Joseph Sohm; ChromoSohm Inc./Corbis; p. 7 © 2002 Geoatlas; p. 9 © Rob Blakers/Getty Images; p. 11 © Historical Picture Archive/Corbis; p. 13 © Chris Hellier/Corbis; pp. 15, 31 (Andrew Jackson) © Stapleton Collection/Corbis; pp. 17, 31 (Fort) © Bettmann/Corbis; p.p. 19, 23 © AP/Wide World Photos; p. 21 © Michael T. Sedam/Corbis; p. 30 (Yellow Jessamine) © Hal Horwitz/Corbis; p. 30 (Great Carolina Wren) © Academy of Natural Sciences of Philadelphia/Corbis; p. 30 (The Palmetto State, Cabbage Palmetto) © Paul A. Souders/Corbis; p. 31 (Calhoun) © The Corcoran Gallery of Art/Corbis; p. 31 (Gillespie) © William Coupon/Corbis; p. 31 (Bethune) © Corbis; p. 31 (Kitt) © John Springer Collection/Corbis; p. 31 (Jesse Jackson) © Marko Shark/Corbis; p. 31 (Farmland) © Owen Franken/Corbis; p. 31 (Swamp) © David Muench/Corbis.

Library of Congress Cataloging-in-Publication Data

Way, Jennifer.
  South Carolina / Jennifer Way ; traducción al español, María Cristina Brusca. — 1st ed.
    p. cm. — (The bilingual library of the United States of America)
  Includes bibliographical references and index.
  ISBN 1-4042-3106-4 (library binding)
  1. South Carolina–Juvenile literature. I. Title. II. Series.
  F269.3.W39 2006
  975.7—dc22
                                                                        2005026284

Manufactured in the United States of America

Due to the changing nature of Internet links, Editorial Buenas Letras has developed an online list of Web sites related to the subject of this book. This site is updated regularly. Please use this link to access the list:

http://www.buenasletraslinks.com/ls/southcarolina

Contents

Contenido

Welcome to South Carolina

South Carolina is known as the Palmetto State. The cabbage palmetto is South Carolina's state tree. You can see the tree on the state flag.

Bienvenidos a Carolina del Sur

Carolina del Sur es conocido como el Estado de la Palmera. La palmera sabal de Carolina es el árbol del estado de Carolina del Sur. Puedes ver esta palmera en la bandera del estado.

South Carolina Flag and State Seal

Bandera y escudo de Carolina del Sur

South Carolina Geography

South Carolina is in the southeast. South Carolina borders the states of North Carolina and Georgia. South Carolina also borders the Atlantic Ocean.

Geografía de Carolina del Sur

Carolina del Sur está ubicado en el sureste del país. Carolina del Sur linda con los estados de Carolina del Norte y Georgia. Carolina del Sur también linda con el océano Atlántico.

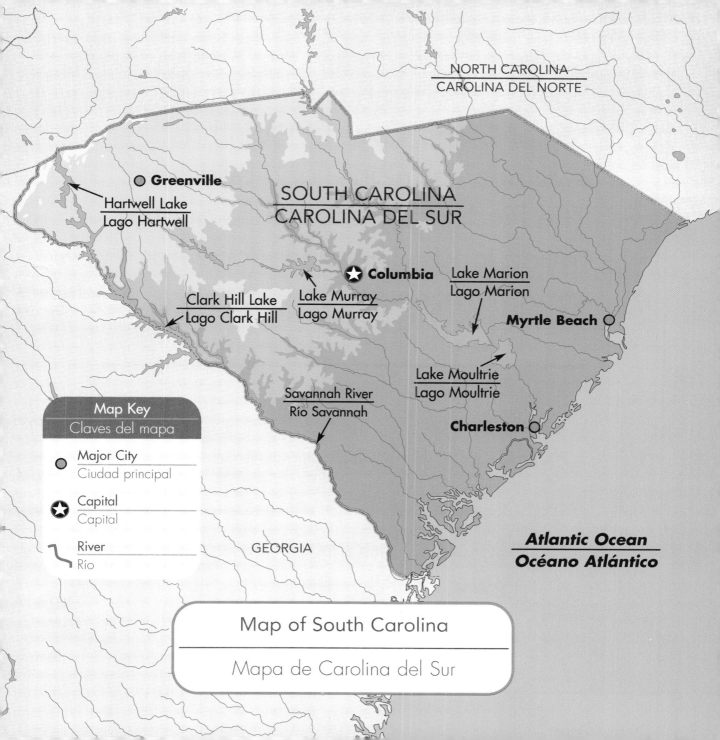

NORTH CAROLINA
CAROLINA DEL NORTE

SOUTH CAROLINA
CAROLINA DEL SUR

Greenville

Hartwell Lake
Lago Hartwell

Columbia

Lake Murray
Lago Murray

Lake Marion
Lago Marion

Clark Hill Lake
Lago Clark Hill

Myrtle Beach

Lake Moultrie
Lago Moultrie

Savannah River
Río Savannah

Charleston

Map Key
Claves del mapa

Major City
Ciudad principal

Capital
Capital

River
Río

GEORGIA

Atlantic Ocean
Océano Atlántico

Map of South Carolina

Mapa de Carolina del Sur

South Carolina has three major regions. The Coastal Plain has swamps, farmland, and beaches. The Piedmont Plateau has gently rolling lands. The Blue Ridge has streams, rivers, and mountains.

Carolina del Sur tiene tres regiones principales. La Llanura Costera tiene terrenos de cultivo, pantanos y playas. La Meseta del Piedmont tiene terrenos ondulantes. El Blue Ridge tiene montañas, ríos y arroyos.

The Appalachian Mountains

Los Montes Apalaches

South Carolina History

The first people to live in South Carolina were Native American groups, such as the Catawba and the Cherokee. Spanish explorers first arrived in South Carolina in 1526.

Historia de Carolina del Sur

Los primeros pobladores de Carolina del Sur fueron grupos de indígenas americanos como los Catawba y los Cheroquí. Los exploradores españoles llegaron al estado en 1526.

Native North Americans in South Carolina

Nativos norteamericanos en Carolina del Sur

South Carolina is named for England's King Charles I. *Carolus* is the Latin name for "Charles." Charles I gave permission to British colonists to settle the area in 1629.

El estado se llama Carolina del Sur en honor a Carlos I, rey de Inglaterra. En latín, *Carolus* quiere decir "Carlos". En el año 1629, los colonos ingleses obtuvieron del rey Carlos I el permiso para establecerse en esta región.

King Charles I (1600–1649)
—————————————
Rey Carlos I (1600-1649)

Francis Marion was a general in the American Revolution. His nickname was the "Swamp Fox" because he led colonial troops through South Carolina's swampy lowlands.

Francis Marion fue un general de la Guerra de Independencia. Adquirió el sobrenombre de "Zorro de los Pantanos" por guiar a las tropas coloniales a través de las tierras bajas y pantanosas de Carolina del Sur.

General Francis Marion (1732–1795)

The Civil War began at Fort Sumter, South Carolina, on April 12, 1861. South Carolina had broken away from the United States. Fort Sumter belonged to the United States and the South fought to take control of it.

La Guerra Civil comenzó en el Fuerte Sumter, en Carolina del Sur, el 12 de abril de 1861. Carolina del Sur se había separado de los Estados Unidos. El Fuerte Sumter pertenecía a los Estados Unidos y el Sur luchó para conservar su control.

Fort Sumter After the Bombing of 1863

Fuerte Sumter después del bombardeo de 1863

Living in South Carolina

South Carolina is famous for barbecue-style cooking, a type of cooking famous in the southern states. People from all over come to South Carolina to sample its food.

La vida en Carolina del Sur

Carolina del Sur es famoso por sus barbacoas, un tipo de cocina tradicional de los estados del sur. Gente de todas partes visita Carolina del Sur para disfrutar de sus platos típicos.

Cooking Barbecue, South Carolina

Barbacoa al horno, en Carolina del Sur

South Carolina is a popular travel spot. Many people come to relax on the state's beaches. Some of the most famous beaches are Myrtle Beach and Hilton Head Island.

Carolina del Sur es un sitio turístico muy popular. Mucha gente disfruta y se relaja en las playas del estado. Dos de sus playas más famosas son Myrtle Beach y Hilton Head Island.

Myrtle Beach, South Carolina

Myrtle Beach, Carolina del Sur

The EdVenture Children's Museum in Columbia, South Carolina, is the largest children's museum in the South. It is filled with fun, hands-on activities in which kids can explore science and nature.

El Museo Infantil EdVenture en Columbia, Carolina del Sur, es el museo infantil más grande en el Sur. En este museo los niños pueden explorar ciencia y naturaleza de manera interactiva.

EdVenture Children's Museum

Museo infantil EdVenture

Columbia, Charleston, and Greenville are the biggest cities in South Carolina. Columbia is the capital of South Carolina.

Columbia, Charleston y Greenville son las ciudades más grandes de Carolina del Sur. Columbia es la capital de Carolina del Sur.

Capitol Building in Columbia, South Carolina
Capitolio en Columbia, Carolina del Sur

Activity:
Let's Draw South Carolina's Flag

Actividad:
Dibujemos la bandera de Carolina del Sur

1

Draw a rectangle.

Dibuja un rectángulo.

2

Add the Moon by making two curved lines.

Agrega la luna trazando dos líneas curvas.

3

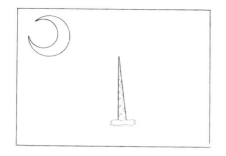

Draw the palmetto tree by making straight and squiggly lines.

Dibuja la palmera sabal trazando líneas rectas y en zigzag.

4

Add the details to the trunk of the tree. Draw the branches.

Agrega detalles al tronco de la palmera. Dibuja las palmas.

5

Color in the flag.

Colorea la bandera.

Timeline

		Cronología
The Carolina colony is divided into North and South.	**1712**	La colonia Carolina se divide en Norte y Sur.
Yamasee Indian War is fought.	**1715**	Se produce la Guerra India Yamasee.
South Carolina becomes a royal colony.	**1721**	Carolina del Sur se convierte en colonia real.
Charles Town is occupied during the American Revolution.	**1781**	Charles Town es ocupado durante la Guerra de Independencia.
The South Carolina capital is moved from Charleston to Columbia.	**1786**	La capital de Carolina del Sur se muda de Charleston a Columbia.
South Carolina breaks away from the United States.	**1860**	Carolina del Sur se separa de los Estados Unidos.
Confederate forces open fire on Fort Sumter, South Carolina, and the Civil War begins.	**1861**	Comienza la Guerra Civil, cuando los Confederados abren fuego sobre el Fuerte Sumter, en Carolina del Sur.
South Carolina rejoins the United States three years after the end of the Civil War.	**1868**	Carolina del Sur se une nuevamente a los Estados Unidos, tres años después del fin de la Guerra Civil.
A popular dance called the Charleston begins in Charleston.	**1925**	Comienza en Charleston un baile muy popular llamado el *charleston*.
Hurricane Hugo causes billions of dollars' worth of damage along South Carolina's coast.	**1989**	El huracán Hugo causa destrucción y pérdidas de billones de dólares a lo largo de la costa de Carolina del Sur.

South Carolina Events/
Eventos en Carolina del Sur

January
Lowcountry Oyster Festival, Mount Pleasant

February
Native Islander Gullah Celebration,
Hilton Head Island
African-American Experience
at Redcliffe, Beech Island

March
Irish Ceili, Columbia
Native American Pow Wow, Hardeeville
Canadian-American Days Festival, Myrtle Beach
Triple Crown Road Races, Aiken

April
Charleston Lowcountry Cajun Festival,
James Island

May
Charleston Greek Fest, Charleston
Foothills Barbecue Festival

June
Watermelon Festival, Hampton

September
South Carolina Apple Festival, Westminster

October
Apple Harvest Festival, York
South Carolina State Fair, Columbia
Chicora Indian Nation Pow Wow, Marion

Enero
Festival de las ostras, en Mount Pleasant

Febrero
Celebración Gullah de los isleños nativos,
en Hilton Head Island
Experiencia afroamericana,
en Redcliffe Beach Island

Marzo
Ceili irlandés, en Columbia
Pow wow nativoamericano, en Hardeeville
Festival canadiense-americano, en Myrtle Beach
Triple corona de turismo de carretera, en Aiken

Abril
Festival cajún de las Tierras Bajas de
Charleston, en James Island

Mayo
Fiesta griega de Charleston, en Charleston
Festival de la barbacoa Foothills

Junio
Festival de la sandía, en Hampton

Septiembre
Festival de la manzana, en Westminster

Octubre
Festival de la cosecha de la manzana, en York
Feria del estado, en Columbia
Pow wow de la nación india Chicora, en Marion

South Carolina Facts/Datos sobre Carolina del Sur

Population
4.1 million

Población
4.1 millones

Capital
Columbia

Capital
Columbia

State Motto
Animis Opibusque Parati,
Prepared in mind and resources,
Dum Spiro Spero,
While I breathe, I hope

Lema del estado
Animis Opibusque Parati:
Listos en cuerpo y alma
Dum Spiro Spero:
Mientras respire tengo esperanza

State Flower
Yellow jessamine

Flor del estado
Jazmín amarillo

State Bird
Great Carolina wren

Ave del estado
Reyezuelo Gran Carolina

State Nickname
The Palmetto State

Lema del Estado
El Estado de la Palmera

State Tree
Cabbage Palmetto

Árbol del estado
Palmera sabal de Carolina

State Song
"Carolina"

Canción del estado
"Carolina"

Famous South Carolinians/
Surcarolinos famosos

**Andrew Jackson
(1767–1845)**

U.S. president
Presidente de E.U.A.

**John C. Calhoun
(1782–1850)**

U.S. vice president
Vice presidente de E.U.A.

**John Birkes 'Dizzy'
Gilespie (1917–1993)**

Jazz musician
Músico de jazz

**Mary McLeod Bethune
(1875–1955)**

Educator and activist
Educadora y activista

**Eartha Kitt
(1927–   )**

Actress and singer
Actriz y cantante

**Jesse Jackson
(1941–   )**

Civil rights leader
Líder de los derechos civiles

Words to Know/Palabras que debes saber

border
frontera

farmland
tierras de cultivo

fort
fuerte

swamp
pantano

Here are more books to read about South Carolina:
Otros libros que puedes leer sobre Carolina del Sur:

In English/En inglés:

South Carolina: The History of an American State
by Horne, Paul A., Klein, Patricia H.
Clairmont, 2000

South Carolina (Hello USA)
by Fredeen, Charles
First Avenue Editions, 2002

Words in English: 305

Palabras en español: 361

Index

Índice